CODE NAME: SHADOW ORIGINS!

ROBB ROURKE

TABLE OF CONTENTS

CODE NAME: SHADOWS ORIGINS

EXECUTIVE SERVICES!

12/16/2016

Briefing with President-elect Jefferson Chase III, at his Chase Plaza Penthouse: New York City, New York.

A delegation from the Intelligence Community flew up to New York from Andrews Air Force Base, to brief the new President on global occurrences. The briefing started cautiously, but smoothly as they compared notes as to policy of the new Administration.

The President-elect looked more like the King on his throne, than an incoming President, as he presided over the briefing. He looked rather uncomfortable **WITHIN THE SHADOWS,** and a bit bored, "...just sitting there and not dealing out the terms of a deal."

"Director Perry, while I respect the reason for this briefing. I ask, as you are the most senior of the Intel. Community, "Why does this Administration need Intelligence?"

A quick pause as he looked at his colleagues, who all got the impression that the President-elect had a disdain for the work of the Intelligence Community, and responded, "Sir, I can give you the company line, but I rather realistic and respond that it is our mission act like a first line of defense against foreign aggression, period!"

Now it was the President-elect's turn to look around the room, as he observed the delegation of Intell Heads. "Well, let me say that while I have no use for the bureaucracy that has built up
over the decades. I'd rather not deal with you, and from now on if there is something My Administration needs to know, report to my Chief of Staff, Bradford Hardy!"

Bradford Hardy was not only the Administration's Chief of Staff designate, he was also the President-elect's Son-in-Law. His only experience with intelligence was working with the President-elect.

The briefing didn't last much longer after these comments from the new President. On the flight back to Washington, Colonel Perry, Head of the FBI, and the Director of National Intelligence talked amongst themselves and expressed concern as to their new boss and his disdain for their work. Interrupting the Director of Intelligence, "... this newbie doesn't think too much about the job we do?" The FBI Director added, "Remember we work at his discretion!" "But, we don't have to like it," added an angry Colonel Perry.

Langley, Virginia: Central Intelligence Agency, Office of Colonel Thomas Perry, Director.

In his usual spot, Chief of Staff Hamilton Jenkins awaited the Colonel's entrance. What he wasn't ready for was the Colonel's anger over the briefing with the President-elect.

The door opened, with such force, the hinge's shook as the Colonel entered and proceeded to his chair. As he sat down, the Colonel reached for a cigar, (note he only lit and smoked his stogie when the Company won a battle of intelligence or was royally mad!) This time, he bit off the end of the cigar and spit it in a waste bucket about twenty feet from his desk. Sat down and proceeded to light it! A few quick breaths and turned to Hamilton, who responded, "That bad, Sir...?" Slamming his attaché on the desk top, knocking over a family picture or two replied, "Damn him! How in the Sam Hill get elected?"

Cautiously easing back in his chair Hamilton inquired again," Didn't go too well, Sir?" Colonel Perry's response, a cold stare that would have sent chills down the spine of the most experienced operative....

"The President-elect has no interest in intelligence," was the Colonel's growling response.

"He has no interest in intelligence! He left the briefing to his Chief of Staff, Bradford Hardy..." Interrupting Hamilton asked, "Isn't that his Son-in-Law, Sir?"
"YES!"

Hamilton, being with the Colonel for over twenty years, knew when it was time for the Colonel to ease down and rethink his options!

After a couple of hours, Hamilton was summoned back to the Colonel's office. "Yes, Sir?" was the response as He sat down opposite his Superior.

Leaning back in his chair, looking like he was pondering a thought, the Colonel asked, "Do you remember 'Air America,' during the Vietnam War?" And with a sense of curiosity, Hamilton replied, "Yes?"

(* Note: Air America, was a legitimate operation/ business with stock sold in the stock market, run through the CIA during the Vietnam War. ror)

What if we set up an operation similar to "Air America," but have a select group of operatives that will truly operate in the

shadows and go where our intelligence cannot go..."
In other words,
"Sacrificial Lambs Sir?"
"No, they will get limited covert assistance, but otherwise on their own!"

"Ham, we have an administration that has issues with us and frankly, this is a mission to fight for!"

"Okay, then what do you mean by limited assistance, Sir,"

"Well, if I am correct, most field operatives have secure storage facilities around the globe. We just need to keep them supplied. Through a third party, who we indirectly control, and won't ask too many questions?" was the Colonel's response.

Leaning back in his chair, Hamilton paused and inquired, "… and who is your first choice for a team member?"

"Carson Towns"

"RIPCORD?"

"And I'm heading to Texas! Have my plane ready and I'll see you at Reagan within the hour!"

It was about three o'clock in the afternoon, (Texas Standard Time) when Carson Towns unlocked the front door of his historical district home on Galveston Island, to Find

Colonel Perry and his Chief of Staff Hamilton Jenkins.

"Come in Carson, we need to talk," greeted the Colonel as he motioned Carson to a comfortable chair. "You could have written..." was the response Carson gave as he sat down.

"We need to talk! I have some work for you!"

TO BE DETERMINED!

CODE NAME: RIPCORD

DICKEN'S ENCOUNTER

(AUTHOR'S NOTE: *THE FOLLOWING TEASE IS THE DICKENS ENCOUNTER! A CLANDESTINE MEETING BETWEEN EAST AND WEST AT A CHRISTMAS FESTIVAL ALONG THE STRAND HISTORICAL DISTRICT, IN GALVESTON, TEXAS.*)

DAY I: 14 DECEMBER, 2018

MOSCOW CENTER: OFFICE OF NEWLY APPOINTED HEAD OF THE OFFICE OF INTERNAL SECURITY (KGB), GENERAL KRASKO.

The General was sitting behind his desk reading over the daily intelligence, "White papers," (INTELLIGENCE REPORTS) when his Chief-Of-Staff burst into the office. He was quickly motioned to a Spartan-like chair opposite the General.

Krasko, newly appointed head of Internal Security quietly worked his way up the ranks of Putin's Russia. "Well, Comrade Chief-Of Staff, and new and important traffic, I need to know about?"

"Well, yes sir. Markov seeks permission to meet once again with the American.

Leaning forward the General inquired, "Comrade, once again brief me as to Markov's assignment and purpose."

"The assignment was to simply put it pass false intelligence to the Americans." "The Cold War is over, right?" asked the General. "Yes, but the President wants it done!"

"Well, then let's make this meeting a bit more interesting," replied the New KGB Chief.

DAY I: HOURS LATER. CIA HEAD QUARTERS: LANGLEY, VA.

Pushing back his chair, the Colonel rose from his desk and walked over to a chess board, purposefully in a spot of distinction. "This new Head of their Intelligence, Let's make sure it will be a lesson well, learned!" ordered the Colonel, who then tactfully moved his chess piece, a pawn, from Queen 1 to Queen 2.

"And make sure our insurance policy is in place," he also added.

The scenario was in place, and the actor's cast for their parts in this drama. The only thing was to see if the plot would thicken?

MOSCOW CENTER

General Krasko, like his American Counterpart, walked over to a chess board and causally move his pawn; "King 1 to King 3."

Alexander Markov, Military Attaché to the Russian Ambassador to the U.N., was the New York, K.G.B. Station Chief, Diplomatic Corps., Third Directorate. He had worked his way through the Russian Intelligence Community in a short period of time, taking this on this assignment personally from the President.

The place of the meeting was to be Galveston, Texas and the time was during the Dickens Christmas Weekend, on the Island. To the Islander's it was the start of the Christmas Season. To the two Spies it was business as usual.

Maria Dunbar, A veteran operative of the Agency. She got the nickname of "Mighty

Mouse," from Carson Towns, simply because of her height and spunk. Maria didn't mind being called, "Mighty Mouse," as long as Carson was the only one to call her that. (She had a bit of a crush on Carson Towns.)

DAY II

Galveston, Texas. December 15, 2018,

Home of Carson Towns.

Lounging on the balcony of his east end home, Carson Towns heard a familiar tune playing; it was Langley with an assignment. Being his first assignment as a member of the EXECUTIVE SERVICES UNIT, he was a bit anxious to what danger can he get into? The theme playing as he quickly made his way to his computer was a favorite from a Clint Eastwood movie, "The Good, The Bad and The Ugly!"

To Carson this theme was a bit of a joke. Officially, he was a disgraced operative forced into retirement. Unofficially, he was reassigned to "the EXECUTIVE SERVICES UNIT!"

Their assignments were dangerous and deniable by the Washington, if compromised.

After a couple of key strokes on the keyboard Carson accepted the assignment and was debriefed. A bit disappointed to be acting as," a Babysitter," but it was an assignment, something short and sweet for he had an invite for Christmas with his brother and family, for the first time in years.

DAY IV

DECEMBER 17, 2018

Within minutes of each other both planes carrying Maria from Dulles and Markov's from Kennedy, their eventual destination Galveston, Texas and an encounter on the Strand.

DAY V

DECEMBER 18, 2018

The day of the festival was at hand and Carson's assignment was to shadow the meeting and keep an eye open for any possible trouble.

Carson arrived early to set up a position near the entrance to take photos of the vast array of Victorian character's celebrating the start of the Christmas Season. Maria Dunbar arrived first followed by Markov a few minutes later. Carson snapped a few pictures of this odd couple of Spies. He momentarily lost them in the crowd and then found them again, next to the outside stairs of the Historical Society Headquarters'.

Suddenly, a queer feeling came over Carson. It was a feeling that he hadn't sensed in a long while. He paused, and scanned the area. Still feeling uneasy he decided to get a better view Carson decided to check out the landscape via his camera lens.

Upon a rooftop, a block and a half west of the Historical District Carson spotted a barrel of a sniper rifle barrel. Quickly, he snapped a few fast shots and then turned toward Maria. With caution and speed, he ran the maze of street urchins, musicians, and tourists, as it was his mission to watch over," Mighty Mouse." Each step seemed as if his feet were glued to the pavement for time was of the essence.

With surprise and timing Carson pushed Maria and Markov up the concrete stairs, as the first shots whizzed by.

With confusion and chaos in full control Maria and Markov responded in unison as more shots rang out, "What the Hell....?", but in two clear and distinct languages. "No time for small talk Mighty Mouse. We need to get out of here!" was the reply as Carson handed her his spare 9mm Heckler and Koch. He then ordered both of them to get ready to make a break for it. Carson pulled out the flash attachment of his camera and yelled, "RUN!"

Aiming for the rooftop, Carson jammed down on the flash. It was his hope to momentarily blind the sniper. Sirens were blaring, panic all along the Strand as Maria and

Markov just made it to safety. Carson soon followed, getting lost in the crowd.

DAY VI

19 DECEMBER, 2018.

<u>MOSCOW CENTER.</u>

As the General read the reports of events in Galveston, he happened to glance over to the chessboard to see his pawn on its side. Suddenly a message flashed on his computer;

ONE CAN ALWAYS LEARN HOW TO PLAY THE GAME. BUT IT TAKES A MASTER TO LEARN HOW TO WIN AND HOW TO ACCEPT DEFEAT...

My regards to the President!

CODE NAME:RIPCORD
WILL RETURN

ASSIGNMENT;

SWISS MOVEMENT

(Author's Note:

Many years ago, it was noted that Super Computer technology, that was sold to the government of Norway was being diverted to Russia. ROR)

The News reports and Social Media went with a full out blitz as the news of ARCOS was passing supercomputer technology to Russia.

The purchase of this software was meant for both the Swiss Military and Swiss Banking Industry.

In Langley, Virginia at CIA Headquarters, Colonel Perry asked his Chief of Staff, Hamilton Jenkins to go in his place as Smid was set to fly into Reagan Airport for Testimony before the Senate Banking and Commerce Committee(s). The Colonel was set to attend an Intelligence Committee meeting at the same time.

Hamilton left Langley about mid -morning and arrived at Reagan about noon and waited in The V.I.P. Suite for Smids' flight from Geneva to land.

What was not known was a meeting between the President of Russia, who at one-time was the Head of Internal Security, KGB, and the new Head of Internal Security, General Ivan Krasko, and a special guest, Edgar LeClerc, The

Raven. With approving eyes, the Russian President just observed the meeting and listened to General Kraskos' briefing of the situation. "While we are in the process of completing our investigation, we need all sources to be silenced!"

"Understood," Was the Raven's only comment as he rose from his chair grabbed the folder given to him and quickly left the smallish office.

He then looked at the President who chose to leave as well, not saying a word. Now the General felt a sense of uneasiness as the President, according to rumors could be considered his most dangerous if he doesn't comment....

The 757 Jumbo Jet, American Airlines taxied to the gate around 1:30 p.m. est. and after disembarking Nicholas Smid was met and escorted to the secure V.I.P. Suite where Hamilton was waiting. Upon entering the two shook hands and quickly sat down and discussed the events of the next couple of days in D.C., when the secure door burst open and shots rang out as the Raven shot at his targets. Smid died instantly with a shot to the forehead. Hamilton was severely wounded in his upper chest.

And as quickly as he entered, the Raven was gone.

Alarms sounded and security soon followed as the airport was now thrown into chaos. Hamilton was evaluated and quickly escorted to the awaiting ambulance. The nearest hospital was George Washington University, where he spent the next several hours in surgery.

In Washington, at the Intelligence Committee meeting the Colonel was informed of events at Reagan and after an exchange of notifying the committee the meeting was adjourned, so assessments and intelligence could be formulated and a strategy to this scenario be in place.

On his way back to Langley, the Colonel was making his own response. First, head for the hospital. Second, check with security from the airport and third, notify Carson Towns that he had an assignment.

Carson was once again sitting on the front porch when he got a call from Hunter J. Wilkens III, head of Trans Global Insurance, Carson's cover, as an Insurance Investigator. The conversation was short and sweet as He prepared for a flight to Hobby airport in Houston to D.C. and then Geneva, Switzerland.

He packed lite, but enough for the cold.

His first call was to a buddy at Scholes Field where he stored his new toy a Cessna airplane. Carson just made the purchase just a couple of months prior, to look the plane the usual once over as he was planning to fly to Hobby Airport to make his flight to Washington.

t was a short flight from Galveston to Hobby, but again this was Carson's new toy! Once landed and the Cessna secured

Carson made his way to the main terminal, where he checked in for his flight.

Once through security Carson headed is to the departure gate and waited to board. The wait was short and the line onto the plane was rather quick. The door was shut and secured as the attendants worked at their final prep before takeoff. Soon the large 757 was allowed to pull away from the terminal and taxi across the tarmac to the runway.

After a couple of minutes waiting their turn the big jet powered its engines and rumbled down the runway and into the bright blue skies.

After about ten minutes in the air the attendants came around asking about drinks. When it came his turn, Carson looked at the pretty young attendant and replied with his drink order, "Vodka martini, shaken, not stirred," with a slight chuckle to his voice. The attendant paused momentarily before she repeated the line. "I always wanted to say that…., "Carson added with a bit of a smirk. "That's good, Mr. Bond…" was her reply.

A couple of minutes passed before she re-appeared with his martini. "Here, you go Mr. Bond…"with a smile on her face placed the drink on the fold down tray. As she walked away pushing her cart, Carson couldn't help from watching her. A quick taste and Carson, thought aloud," … not bad at all, Mr. Bond you have something here…." He then noticed the napkin and a short note that consisted of her, Nancy Evans and her phone number. Quickly Carson tapped the number into the memory of his smartphone...

The flight to Washington took just under two hours. Carson made his way through the crowded airport to security, where he was able to quickly look over the security footage. And right away Carson spotted him, Edgar LeClerc, the Raven the suite, shooting out the security cameras. He talked with security and asked about security as with the press and other media that may show up at the hospital.

Carson then quickly grabbed a cab and headed to George Washington University Hospital in the Foggy Bottom area of Washington.

Upon arrival at the hospital Carson made his way to Hamilton's room except to find him in intensive care and no one except medical personnel were admitted. Carson noticed Colonel Perry sitting alone in a nearby waiting room. With head in his hands the Colonel looked as if he had been praying for his old friend. Slowly Carson approached his ever cantankerous superior.

"Well, Carson finally decided to show up, I see?" "I got here as quickly as I could. I first wanted to checkout any pictures." Sitting

more erect the Colonel responded, "There was security footage?" "Yes Sir, an old Friend, the Raven himself, Edgar LeClerc."

"By the way, how is Ham?" asked a concerned Carson. "Usual line from the Doctor, the next twenty-four hours ...." Well Carson sat with his Old boss with the respect of a son to his father. "Carson, find out how the software was diverted and plug the whole!"

And on that note Carson excused himself and made his way back to Reagan Airport. His flight was to leave around nine p.m. and arrive mid-morning the next day. At the check in desk

Carson inquired as to his ability to upgrade to business class, and the response was yes!

Once again through security and Carson went to his departure gate and waited for his flight. The wait seemed as it was a precursor for the flight to Geneva. Finally, the boarding door opened and passengers were allowed to board. Carson quickly found his seat and got rather comfortable as the seat reminded him of his recliner at home in Galveston.

The Swiss Air 737 Jumbo jet rolled down the runway and quickly lifted its mighty structure into the air and soar off toward their destination of Geneva, Switzerland. The flight was long and the movie was entertaining, but brief. The meal was actually good by airline standards. The attendant made her rounds asking who wanted a pillow. Carson quickly took his and leaned back and was quickly asleep, pondering the adventure ahead of him.

The flight landed about mid- afternoon Geneva time. Upon disembarking Carson quickly made his way through security and to an awaiting taxi, outside. The weather Carson paused as the cold hit like a ton of bricks. He was dressed for the cold, but not this cold. He quickly instructed the cabbie to drive him to the Hotel Warwick Geneva. The hotel was located near a smallish shopping area where Carson could get a few extra items to fight off the cold he was feeling.

The ride was rather short and the scenery was very picturesque for this was Carson's first trip to the Swiss Capital.

After a quick check in at the Warwick, Carson was escorted to his room on the 5th floor by a bellhop that gave off a look that he may know a bit more than house rules allowed, making note of Carson room.

Carson relaxed for a while as to get a lay of the land as he tried to work off the jet lag. As quick as the sun rose that morning, it set just as fast, and from his window Carson, look out upon the frozen sheen of what could be described as a sheet of diamond chips as the snow glowed in the early evening air. Still feeling a bit tired from his flight, Carson ordered a small salad, with Italian dressing from room service and prepared for bed and a good night sleep. The next day was to be a long one as Carson was to spend a good portion of the day at ARCOS, and any free time after the fact he would be buying a few warmer clothes to fight the Cold.

The morning sun worked its way through the French doors and finally covered the bed where Carson slept. Slowly rising Carson felt a real need to get warm really quick. Hurrying into the bathroom he started a rather hot shower where the stiffness of the flight seemed to ease in just minutes. After soaping himself up and then washing down Carson just leaned back and enjoyed the feel of the steam as it engulfed his now, much warmer body. And after the steam, came a quick shave and grab clothes and then breakfast, which consisted of toast local jellies and a big pot of hot Swiss chocolate. Carson was never a big fan of coffee and just *tolerated the hot drink of most Americans. He just enjoyed the sweet taste of chocolate. Yes, he had a bit of a sweet tooth.*

After the last cup Carson, made a quick call asking for a car and driver for he had an appointment in town. Carson was down on to the ground floor in a matter of minutes and out the door to his awaiting limousine and his first stop ARCOS. The ride was long as the driver gave Carson the tour of Geneva, and pointed out some men's shops where he might find some warmer clothing.

In Moscow, at KGB HQ. General Krasko seemed rather frustrated as he had gotten off the phone with the President, who was mad as global and social media were gathering steam pointing an accusing finger at the former Soviet Empire. "Does he not understand he's was the one who, gave the order," the General shouted aloud to his Chief of Staff. "The world saw the Friend Raven shooting out the security camera and somehow the world accuses us! Damn that Social Media."

"Well, remember, in 2016 we were able to help their new President get elected, "replied the Chief of Staff.

At George Washington University Hospital Colonel Perry was discussing Hamilton Jenkins current status. The doctor told him that Hamilton had suffered severe wounds and damaged organs like his lungs and that one bullet was lodged near his

Spinal column. When asked if Hamilton would walk again, the doctor was not sure.

Carson's limo finally drove through the ARCOS gates, where he passed through security and quickly walked into the main building to his appointment. The receptionist escorted him to the office of Acting Chief Executive Officer, Olaf Gerg. He was a man in his upper fifties with a receding hairline and appeared to walk with a limp as he walked from behind his desk to greet Carson.

What Carson did not know that Olaf Gerg was a Russian Asset, operative for the K.G.B. This was the connection as to how the Russian's were able to upgrade their computer technology and cyber spying of the west.

As he directed Carson to a chair opposite his desk Olaf Gerg asked the first question," And what brings you to ARCOS, Mr. Towns?"

"Well, for one thing the death of your CEO, Nicholas Smid, and TransGlobal wants me to investigate his death and the actuation of diverting computer technology to the Russian's," Gerg became a bit rather defensive and the interview progressed.

Carson was able to get confirmation of the company's origin in the mid 60's and ARCOS' place in the Cyber world.

As if out of nowhere Nicholas Smid's daughter, Mia came in to the office. Carson couldn't help from noticing that Gerg seemed rather relieved to see Mia and not answer any more questions.

Gerg quickly introduced Mia to Carson who turned his attentions and questions to the young and very attractive lady to sat next to him.

Mia was in her mid- twenties, short brown hair cut in a style that could easily be called a Beatle cut.

Carson briefly talked with Mia about events from her perspective. Carson surmised that you knew more than she was willing to talk, probably due to the environment of the office. Then of course there was Olaf Gerg. A cold chill went down Carson's spine at that moment, and remembered the cold outside!

After a brief and harsh discussion with the Russian President, General Krasko privately talked about the environment between the Russian President and the recently appointed head of Internal Security. The General felt the wrath of the President over this particular operation. He was the one who brought in the Raven, and the Russian President was trying to regain control over the politics that were allowing the global events that were playing against," Mother Russia!"

The Kremlin had virtually shut down many sources of the global media, but not social media.

At George Washington University Hospital the Colonel basically set of his temporary office in the adjoining area to that of his Chief of Staff, and loyal friend, Hamilton Jenkins. The Colonel was able to monitor flash traffic out of Russia for stress points. What he discovered was a growing divide between the Russian leadership in the Kremlin and the Head of Internal Security.

At ARCOS Mia offered to give Carson a tour of the complex, and answered many for a novice on the computer. "In a world of technology around us 24/7, I must admit to being digitally challenged." Carson responded. The ice shroud that appeared to cover Mia appeared to slip off as he finally heard her laugh at a bad a joke by Carson.

Carson asked Mia if she would have lunch with him and she refused saying that she had to prepare for her father lying in state in the main hall of ARCOS and memorial the following day and funeral.

Then feeling like he put his foot in

his mouth Carson apologized. The twosome made their way to the main entrance where they parted.

Carson made a couple of stops as per the suggestion of the limo driver, where he bought a better and warmer winter coat.

Upon his return to the Warwick and subsequently his room, a knock and upon opening the door Carson found Mia.

"Mr. Towns, I want to apologize for my rudeness. If the offer is still good, I would be glad to share a meal with you." Putting up two reminiscent of Winston Churchill, and FDR, Carson added two things," The name is Carson and do please choose the restaurant for this is my first trip to Switzerland, okay?"

Again, Mia smiled and gave a brief, but hearty chuckle.

Mia indicated that a company car was at their disposal. Carson followed the lead of his young date as she led him downstairs and outside to a vintage Aston Martin DB5. "Holy 007," exclaimed Carson as frozen exhaust was expelled from his lungs. Mia briefly paused and inquired of his response, "I am a big James Bond fan!"

Now giving a hearty laugh, Mia indicated that they should get in the car, to get warmer! The turn of the key; the roar of the engine and Carson felt like a kid in a Candy Store. "Ah, to ride in his Car..." exclaimed Carson. Now a bit puzzled Mia asked, "Excuse me?" This particular Aston Martin was used in the Bond movie, 'GOLDFINGER,'

Mia just laughed and replied, "My mother had an old saying for situations like this,'...boys' with toys', "followed by laughter from both as the Aston Martin left the driveway at the Warwick.

The evening was quiet and ran at a pace that Mia felt comfortable with. The meal was excellent and the conversation

was about her father. What they didn't know was that they were being watched by Olaf Gerg. Gerg was in a bulky SUV not far from the restaurant. As he observed Gerg was in

communication with the Russian President giving him bi-hourly report on his observations. This angered the Russian President, despite the fact he was once head of Internal Security, KGB.

World press and Social Media were making what appeared to be hourly reports of turmoil within the walls of the Kremlin. Did," the Iron Leader," have a chink in his armor?

These thoughts also crossed The Colonel's mind as well. "RIPCORD, you're making him nervous, the Colonel thought aloud, as the Doctor walked in to check on Hamilton.

The Colonel's attention quickly shifted to the Doctor and his observations. "Well, Doctor when will, my Chief of Staff be able to return to work?" he growled...

A pause, followed by, "Sir, in all due respect your Chief of Staff is one lucky Son of a Bitch. What those bullet fragments did to his

body... He shouldn't be alive, but he is, and you want to know when he'll be back... months at the earliest." And on that note the Doctor turned and walked out the front door.

The next morning brought two different meetings; In Moscow General Krasko was summoned once again to the Kremlin for an audience with the President. Upon entering the good General felt a cold chill, but soon realized that he was not outside that was cold that radieted from the Russian President, himself. Not a motion, just silence as General Krasko stood at attention

In Geneva, the morning brought renewed interests in the events of the day, the memorial followed by the burial in the foothills

of the Alps. Carson, made a quick call to the Colonel's secure cell phone. Within a couple of rings, the Colonel answered with his infamous growling," Hello.... Ah nephew how are you doing? Rather quiet Uncle, met a new friend and we've spent a bit of time together so far. As you know with the recent family tragedy everything has been rather quiet. How's cousin?"

"I don't trust those people. They'll wake you up just to give you a sleeping pill!" commented the Colonel. "Your cousin is steadily improving, but it will take months for him to recover. "Okay, just wanted to check on cousin... will check in later," responded Carson and clicked off.

Carson quickly ordered breakfast from room service. Within a few minutes, It was his usual toast, scrambled eggs and hot chocolate.

At KGB Headquarters General Krasko returned to his office where his Chief of Staff was waiting. Taking the General's coat from him and hanging it on the nearby coat rack, the Chief of Staff inquired of the meeting with the President. "My friend, you have known me for how long?" inquired the General. "Thirty-five years, General ..." was the puzzled response. "What is your opinion of me?" He asked. "I feel that you are a fair leader, and respectful superior, Sir?" replied the Chief of Staff.

Reaching over to the intercom on his desk General Krasko ask his secretary to come into his office. "Alexis, please have a seat. I want to dictate a letter....

As he sat down, General Krasko

"Mr. President,

While, I respect your position as the leader of our great country, I must with all sincerity submit my resignation as Head of Internal Security....

within minutes reports of General Krasko's resignation were surfacing in Social Media. This was another chink in the Armor of the Russian President.

The memorial started about 10 a.m. in the main hall of ARCOS, where the casket of Nicholas Smid laid in state. Mia acted as host and greeted the room of invitees. The ceremony lasted an hour.

Meanwhile, many representatives from neighboring Europeans countries expelled many top- level Russian diplomats as the ceremonies were proceeding. As the ceremony was progressing Mia asked Carson to go with her to the burial site, just outside of Lausanne. Carson agreed. As all exited the hall Mia greeted and thanked once again for their time and continued friendship. Then Mia and Carson made their way her awaiting limousine not far from the front end of the complex.

In Moscow, the President made a phone call on a secure line to the Raven, giving him one more order. "The burial is outside of

Lausanne. Wipe it clean!" And the conversation ended.

The ride was a photographer' dream the mixture of snow, Swiss architecture, and children playing in the snow, but many knew of Nicholas Smid and the service he gave for Switzerland. They all stood in respect as the caravan of cars passed by. Carson looked with a sense of amazement, simply because it was something new to him. In a world full of shadows Carson Towns discovered a light in a shadowy world.

As the Caravan was making its way to the burial site no one noticed a shadowy figure on the mountain side about 175 feet up. It was the Raven planting explosive charges and setting the *timer for six minutes. They were interactive as the Raven liked to watch!*

a quick adjustment and the timers were set. The procession of cars slowly made its way to the newly dug burial site over- looking the city of Lausanne. A click of a switch and the timer started its countdown:

5:59:45

A quirky, but sinister smile came across the face of the Raven as he watched the procession drive to its destruction....

5:45:03

Mia inched closer to Carson the procession headed toward the burial site.

4:59:37

4:00:02

3:45:13

2:59:58

2:30:26

28

As the Hearst pulled into the cemetery the explosions went off, causing an avalanche. Panic spread amongst the passenger that followed to the entombment.

Luckily Mia and Carson were secure in their seats as their vehicle was hit by the on rush of snow.

News and Social media reports were circling the globe. At George Washington Hospital the Colonel and Hamilton were shocked by the events as being reported.

As the days past and the reports concerning possible survivors, condemnation of Russia mounted as Embassy employees were expelled from around the world.

Suddenly and almost simultaneously in Moscow and Washington both the Russian President and Colonel Perry received similar boxes. Upon opening each found news clippings of the events and an MP-3 player attachment for Hamilton's laptop. Quickly as if in unison the Colonel and Russian President let the music play: It was Queen's "Another One Bites the Dust!"

Almost doubling over from the laughter Hamilton pronounced, "RIPCORD MADE IT! He's alive!"

The End

ASSIGNMENT;
END AROUND

In that same package that arrived in Hamilton's George Washington University Hospital was a brief note asking to meet with the Colonel in 3 days in Berlin at the American Embassy.

Signed,

General Krasko.

"What the hell?" exclaimed the Colonel as he read the note. Puzzled Hamilton inquired as to the contents of the note.

"From Krasko, he wants to meet... in Berlin, of all places," replied the Colonel.

"Berlin, Sir?" further asked the recovering Chief of Staff.

"I am curious enough to go," responded the Colonel

And if by unison, both the Colonel and Hamilton responded, "He wants to defect? "But Berlin, why?" questioned the Chief of Staff. With a smile on his face, the Colonel replied, "He's a History Buff!" And then added the biggest relic of, "the Cold War, "is Berlin, Germany, and that's where he wants to come over to us!"

31

"So, let's get him a little insurance," walking over to the Samsung notebook that he brought with him during his stay while on vigil at Hamilton's room at George Washington University Hospital. A few taps of the keyboard and a thumb drive in the Colonel's hand was inserted into drive "E", and the Queen song, "Another one Bites the Dust..."

In the Kremlin the Russian President receives a similar box with a similar thumb drive. He also inserted it into the open drive on his laptop computer and to his surprise, "Another One Bites the Dust..." Angered the President rips the thumb drive from the laptop and throws it against the wall. For a man that

took pride in showing how cool and in charge he was allowing things to get under his skin.

Back in D.C. Hamilton, started laughing "RIPCORD, he's alive! He's alive!" The Colonel just stood there, with a smile and shook his head, like a proud papa to his son.

"Then, he can work!" barked the Colonel as he removed the thumb drive and replaced with on from a key bob he carried and placed it in the notebook drive. A few taps of the

keypad and a link to EXECUTIVE SERVICES; a select group of Operatives volunteers to act as a first line of defense against foreign aggression.

Another tap of the keypad and a signal through top secret channels assigned CODE NAME: RIPCORD, Carson Towns on his new assignment.

Carson Towns and Mia Smid were recovering from their avalanche experience going on a couple of weeks after the incident. They were staying in Carson's room at the Warwick Hotel in Geneva when he got the assignment. A quick two knocks on the door and Carson answered to reveal one of the concierges with a large tan envelope. Inside was his

assignment: Shadow General Krasko, formerly head of Internal Security. Possible defection?

Make sure he gets to Berlin, Germany in next 3 days.

As quick as he read the contents of the envelope Carson lit a match and watched as the paper burned into ashes. A look back to Mia lying across the bed with a puzzled look on her face, and he asked if she would like to accompany him into Moscow? Sitting up rather quickly Mia didn't realize that a couple of the buttons on her top popped loose revealing her supple breast. Carson leaned down and rather kiss them he gently re button them and asked if she had a corporate jet and how long would it take to prepare for a flight to Moscow, Russia. Grabbing her

cell Mia made a couple of calls and then replied to Carson, "The Lear jet will be ready within the next two hours." Passport up, to date?" A nod of the head told Carson enough. The twosome was ready to go in a relatively short period of time. A short ride in the elevator and checkout Carson and Mia were in route to a private airstrip. The ride was rather quick as to the time of and light traffic on that cold morning. Upon arrival Carson and Mia quickly boarded the jet. Within a *few minutes the jet was soaring into the skies toward Moscow.*

Their flight plans had them landing at one of Moscow's three airports, Domodedovo Moscow Airport. This particular airport was built during the height of the Cold War and used as a major hub for international flights. It was located roughly forty-two kilometers from Moscow.

In the Kremlin, the Russian President was yelling at anyone to find General Krasko. He just would not accept the fact that he had resigned.

What the President didn't realize that the General was home, with his wife of 25 years, Nadia in their apartment overlooking Gorky Park.

33

The General and Mrs. Krasko discussed their feelings over the idea of defecting. There were differing opinions but, in the end,

both agreed that it was in their best interests to leave as soon as possible!

The Lear jet landed at Domodedovo, about mid- afternoon. Carson and Mia disembarked and quickly made it through airport security. After grabbing a cab Carson, let Mia choose the hotel to stay in. Her choice was the Hotel Novotel Moscow Centre. As they drove up Carson was a bit taken back as to the luxurious look of the Hotel located so near "Ground Zero," during the Cold War, Red Square itself!

Back in George Washington University Hospital, the Colonel pacing back and forth as he waited to see how Hamilton was doing after his first session of therapy. A beep from the

Colonel's phone indicated that Carson Towns was in Moscow and on the job.

Mia and Carson made their way into the grand hotel. Mia would later tease Carson, as to the fact that he looked like a youngster walking down the middle aisle of church, for the first time, before services.

It was a rather grand hotel. It had been a while since Carson's last trip into, "Ground Zero," for Communism during the Cold War. It was a big adjustment to see the influence of the West in the Cold of Mother Russia.

Mia checked in and got them a suite.

After a quick ride up to the tenth floor, and then quick walk to their suite. Carson tipped the bellhop as Mia opened the door and walked in. Carson followed behind carrying the luggage. Once he found a place to drop the luggage Carson removed his jacket, hung it in the closet and fell across the bed where Mia slid next to him. Carson enjoyed Mia lying next to him and unbuttoned a few buttons on his shirt as she removed and proceeded to seduce Carson. They enjoyed and embraced the shared the moments of passion.

And when done Mia asked with a smirk on her face," Was it good for you?"

Carson replied in a bit of a tongue and cheek manner, "007 would be envious!" Looking at him Mia proceeded to grab a pillow and hit him! They laughed and rough housed a bit and fell into each other's arm's sound asleep.

Their sleep was peaceful and passionate. They were tired from the flight and simply were tired from jet lag.

The morning brought the sun into the suite where Carson finding a feather started waving it across the tip of her nose. A quick brush back across her woke Mia up and quickly she took

a swipe at Carson with her pillow across his head. a quick laugh and then making love once again in the hot shower.

After a brisk rubdown with their towels, Carson ordered room service for two; coffee, toast, sausage, and eggs, scrambled for him and poached for her.

Within a few short minutes of receiving breakfast, both Carson and Mia were dressed and headed down the elevator and to the front desk where they could rent a car to get around Moscow.

Their first stop was to park and observe events outside the General's home near Groky Park.

While in route to cross paths with the General, Carson briefly discussed that she could be arrested and held on charges to that could be anything! And she said, "I do not know a thing except we were on vacation and you wanted to show me some of your old haunts," with a rather wide smile!

35

A quick nod of his head and Carson proceeded to pass her a business card with a phone number to a burner cell phone Carson always carried out of habit. "Don't make a show of it, but try and pass this card to the General and we do trips to Berlin, and disappear, as quick as possible!" "You mean get to the car, as quick as possible?" she inquired. "No, the hotel

and try not to get noticed!" Carson replied in a stern manner. "I will be observing the area for quick exit routes. Oh, yeah make sure your jet is ready on a moment's notice to get the hell out of Dodge!"

Mia, looked as if she just had her first session of basic training as a field operative. "Wait a minute, I will be in the open and alone doing this?" she once again asked like an inquiring mind.

"I'll be near at all times. You see, I'll be the first option as they know who I am for my work for the government a while back,"replied Carson. A pause and then the inquiring mind of Naive Mia asked, with a smirk on her face, "So, you were a spy?"

"That's highly classified!" was the response with a similar smirk!

They prepared for the cold weather of the Moscow winter and then made their way to the first floor. There they made an inquiry of car rentals and the manager directed them to a hertz counter where Carson rented a smallish" SUV," from Kia and got a map of the city where Carson studied as he walked back to Mia. A quick walk to the rental storage area was a real necessity as, despite the winter clothing were still cold. A click of the car bob and the locked SUV became unlocked. Another click and the engine roared. Carson quickly turned the heat on as Mia shifted gears and pulled the vehicle out of its parking space and drove out of the area and on to the streets of Moscow.

36

The traffic was light, but surprisingly slow. For conversation purposes Mia inquired what her role was in this secret mission. Carson replied that she was to observe then when the time was right to pass a simple business card to the General. Carson then gave her the card. On one side was a picture of Churchill, Roosevelt, and Stalin. The front side picture was a universal sign of friendship and trust amongst allies. The other side was a cell phone number that was a link to Langley and reconnected back to Carson own cell phone.

As they got closer to the General's apartment, just outside Gorky Park, Carson instructed Mia to park and he would get out to shadows the General. As Carson made his way from the SUV he couldn't help being reminded of the Cold War Era, the ongoing battle between the Soviet Union and the Western Allies.

As he breathed the cold air in and out he pondered this thought, "Well, Mister Bond what next?" A quick chuckle and Carson quickly found a nondescript spot for him to observe. Within a

few minutes The General appeared walking his Husky Max. A quick tapping on the keys of his cell and Mia's phone rang...

She answered and followed Carson's instruction to follow the General for about a block or two from across the street. After about twenty minutes he would need her to re-cross the street and then bump into the General and plant the card where he could easily find it. She nodded and proceeded. She followed a parallel path to that of the General. She and Carson were communicating with their blue tooth devices, so interruptions.

Suddenly, Carson ordered her to go up a block up and double back on the General's side of the street. The General and Max had briefly stopped as Max needed to relieve himself. Carson observed Mia making her way back toward the General and Max. And before he could respond Mia had bumped into the General and Max. She petted Max and Shook the General's hand *as she passed the card over to him. He looked a little puzzled and Mia Commented, "Message from a friend. Berlin trip extremely possible, "and then walked off toward the SUV.*

Shaking his head Carson felt a bit amazed and commented, "She's no Honey chili Rider, but..." and made his way back to the SUV.

Carson and Mia took the scenic route back to the hotel. They spent the next few hours waiting for the phone to ring...

Carson turned the stereo on as he asked Mia to dance. It was a slow dance of passion as Mia and Carson began removing

clothing as the cellphone rang. "Timing," was Carson's only response as he accepted the call. "Yes Sir..."

let's say that I am a friend and you need my help!" The voice on the other end of the call acknowledged the subject matter of the

conversation. "Berlin, two days?" Carson replied as he turned in Mia's direction. Quickly, she responded by calling her pilot and requesting that the Lear jet be in a state of readiness Turning back to the cell conversation Carson proceeded to instruct the General needed to do, " don't pack and be ready to move on a moment's notice. and the meet up spot will be the same general area where you briefly met my associate, this morning."

And the call ended!

Turning back to Mia, Carson responded, "Your jet 24 to 48 hour's notice, Okay?" As he quickly and kissed her in an intimate manner. This was followed by their two bodies lying across the sheets slowly removing each other's remaining clothing as the seduction continued. They made love a number of times during the evening, making it a beautiful night of

A peacefully, slow evening of waiting by the phone for a call that may never happen.

38

Mia fell asleep in Carson's arm's, and as she woke the next morning she found Carson dressing, " Did I miss something?" the pretty, but half a sleep beauty asked, as she tried to wipe the sleep from her eyes. "Old habits, but when there's an extraction one needs to be ready on a moment's notice. The General knows that and he is probably been ready to go before we leave this hotel. So, get dressed and let's get the hell out of Dodge, okay?"

Without a response Mia was dressed, packed and ready to go.

Carson and Mia then proceeded downstairs and to checkout.

Carson rented a new car and then he and Mia drove to Gorky Park to pick up their companions. Carson instructed Mia to get the jet ready for flight. The conversation lasted a few minutes, and she said that it would be ready to go as soon as they get there!

The ride seemed a bit quicker and easier as the traffic appeared to be almost non-existent. Carson slowed down as he got closer to Gorky Park. Along the pathway Mia spotted the General, his wife and their dog Max. Handing her the phone Carson ordered her to call the General to be ready to make the move. The call went out and the General acknowledged and appeared ready.

Carson made a quick stop and honk of the horn as a signal for the General to come, "NOW!" As quick as the

couple could run in the snow, the General, his wife and Max made it into Carson's rental as KGB operatives appeared out of nowhere!

Shots rang out!

A turn left of the steering wheel was followed by a quick turn right as the car's swayed across the streets wet from the snow and luckily for Carson saw an ice patch and quickly out foxed the KGB driver and his partner as the car crashed into a parked alongside the streets leading to the airport.

39

As the drove on to the airport grounds Carson quickly handed Mia a cellphone and ordered her to call the pilot and crew to be ready to go! "General, please be aware as soon as we stop, we need to move fast and I mean fast, Sir!" Carson shouted to the General.

The rental came to a halt near the entrance of the ARCOS hanger. "OUT! NOW, RUN to the plane." was the order.

Max was the first aboard followed by the General, Mrs. Krasko, Mia and last Carson.

Quickly they found their seats and the plane made a quick exit heading toward the runway. A pause for instructions and when the airport tower refused to respond Carson Gave the order to go, period!

The Lear jet slowly built speed as security vehicles chased after...

Soon the Lear was in the air and the flight to the border began. Some 10 miles outside of Moscow was the first sign of Russian Chase planes ordering the Lear to return to Moscow on order of the Russian President.

Carson, told the pilot," Until you hit the border, radio silence!"

"And if they try to shoot us down?" inquired the pilot. "Avoid it, Period" was the response.

As they inched closer to the Russian border the chase planes continued to order the Lear to return to Moscow. Finally over the radio was the order to shoot the jet down. It was the Russian President barking the orders. The stress of the past few weeks was starting to show signs of panic, and tension.

The first missile sailed by as it purposely missed. "Avoid at all costs and do not panic," Carson instructed the pilot. Another missile quickly soared past as the pilot avoided it. "Good," was the response as Carson approved of the quick move. Suddenly, the co-pilot announced the Polish border was a head.

Carson, turned to the General and asked him to try and calm his wife down and then instructed him to dial a particular number. That was the Colonel's secure and private line. It took the General just a couple of moments before he made contact with Colonel Perry. He passed on a request for a company car at the ExecuJet Company at Airport in Berlin, and the conversation ended. Handing phone back to Carson, the General acknowledged that the company car would be there.

Carson then suggested that the young lady be escorted out of the cockpit and to a seat for it will be a bumpy ride into Germany as the Russian military had a tendency, to ignore borders.

Strapping himself in the co-pilot's seat Carson reminded the pilot to maintain radio silence for now.

The General ordered his wife to buckle up and he secured Max to the best of his ability and then himself, just as the pilot made a quick banking turn away from an air to air missile as it roared past.

The General then dialed the secure number that Carson gave him the Colonel. Two short rings and Colonel Perry answered. "Your Nephew suggested to we need a company car by waiting at the Execu Jet Company at Tempelhof Airport. ETA: hour and a half. The Colonel acknowledged and the conversation was finished.

The General then called out to Carson that everything will be ready at the airport.

Hearing this, the pilot asked, out of curiosity," Tempelhof is where we land?" "No, I just wanted to have the Russian's think that and giving us some time!" was Carson's response.

41

"An old trick," he added with a bit of a smile....

Suddenly one more turn of the jet and another missile soared by just missing, this time closer to the target.

News Media was getting reports of Russian jets chasing and attempting to shoot down a civilian jet as it left Russian Airspace. Air to Air missiles were seen soaring across the eastern region of Poland.

Polish Officials quickly demanded answers to these events from Moscow.

There was no comment from the Kremlin!

As soon as the News Media was sparking the global reaction within the Polish landscape the jets were ordered back to Russia.

Smooth sailing from that point on!. The phone call to the Colonel was not on a secure line as Carson said, but one that

could be easily intercepted by Russian's assigned to their Embassy in Berlin.

And when they arrived with the intent to intercept the flight they would be exposed and later expelled from Germany back to Russia.

Carson and the General briefly spoke as the he thanked Carson for his help.

"Mr. Towns, we can no longer repeat history. We must continue to write a new!"

CODE NAME: RIPCORD

WILL RETURN!

CODE NAME:
RIPCORD
MESSAGE FROM ALLAH!

AUTHOR NOTE:

This is a fictionalized accounting of the days leading up to Iraq's invasion of Kuwait.

DAY I:

TIME PERIOD, JULY 28-AUGUST 02....

It was a rather hot morning in Georgetown, one could almost sense that the August was right around the corner. Ali Abudar, cultural Attaché to the Kuwaiti Embassy, walked out the front door of his condo. And as he drew closer to his new Mercedes Benz, he spun the key bob around his finger of his right hand, until all he had had to do was push a couple of buttons on his remote. Button one unlocked the car door. Button two and the car exploded sending debris in all directions, killing Abudar instantly.

Chaos reigned until first responder's arrived. In the mix of this madness no one noticed a shadowy figure among the crowd that gathered. It was Edgar LeClerc, the infamous Raven. Momentarily viewing the destruction and chaos that he created simply faded into the background, leaving his calling card, with a simple message," The Raven Evermore!"

At Langley, Chief of Staff, Hamilton Jenkins rushed in to the Colonel's office to find him watching the news coverage of the explosion. "This was an assassination, pure and simple, "as he motioned the Chief of Staff into a chair opposite him. "I'm about to ask a rather silly question, Sir, but how do you know it was a bomb?" inquired the puzzled Chief of Staff.

A slow turn away from the television monitor and the Colonel responded, "Look at the blast pattern, and access to the preliminary report that indicates probable bomb." Leaning back in his chair the Colonel then asked, "Any traffic out of the Middle East?" "Will check on it, Sir," was the response.

45

DAY II:

TIME PERIOD JULY 29

THE RETAINER!

It was about 5:30 a.m. in Galveston, Texas when Carson Towns cell phone woke him up, with the Bond Ringer, "Not, early enough, my friend..." as he answered the phone.

"Towns, Towns are you awake?" an impish voice inquired. "Not really sure at the moment," was Carson smirked. On the other end of the conversation was Hunter J. Simpson, IV. "Now, Towns enough of your so-called wit! Mr. Sanderson, your boss of TRANS GLOBAL INSURANCE, has a job for you..."

Carson usually felt that he was a good judge of character and often regarded Hunter a work in progress (Only joking....)

Carson quickly dressed, and packed as he waited for his instructions. The instructions printed in a matter of moments along with airline ticket to Washington. Carson used a car service to head for the airport and while in route he read the reports.

By noon the flight landed at Dulles. Carson quickly passed through security and headed to a car rental service. Found his luggage and headed out for Washington Police.

Upon arrival at police headquarters in Georgetown, Carson was introduced to the investigating officer Bart Tompkins. The courtesy briefing lasted about 20 minutes with Carson being led to the Corners' office, where he was able to see the forensic report concerning the bombing.

Carson's next stop was a hotel where he spent most of the afternoon going over the reports. Suddenly, a call on his cell and it was Hunter Simpson, who informed Carson his next stop was Kuwait City.

Now Carson had a question to ponder, "Why was this man that important to have Edgar, kill him?"

DAY III:

On the Road, Again!

JULY 30

The morning sun rose with a start as it abruptly woke Carson. Finding his bed covered with paper he quickly gathered his reports and packed them in his attaché case. He then showered and dressed as he went down to the dining area for the buffet and headed back to Dulles for his flight to Kuwait.

Without a knock on his door Hamilton Jenkins rushed into the Colonel's office, "Sir, intelligence, from usual sources in Iraq..." Quickly the Colonel motioned his Chief of Staff to a chair and asked, "What?" "Iraqi Troop movement heading in the direction of Kuwait." The Colonel paused momentarily and then responded," First send a flash to our man in Kuwait City. Tell him to check his sources and second, check on RIPCORD'S progress. "

47

First stop was the car rental agency, then the tram to the main part of the Airport, where he passed through security and then headed toward the flight gate. It was a short wait before his flight was called for Kuwait City.

The Kuwaiti Airbus slowly rolled across the tarmac and then on to its assigned runway. As the thrust increased pushing the Airbus forward Carson let his mind wander to anything but current affairs. He remembered being introduced to the idea of joining EXECUTIVE SERVICE, a small select group of operatives, permanently assigned for highly dangerous missions. Highly classified and very deniable by the government.

Other memories that briefly arose to his conscious were that of Natalia and the brief moment of her death.

The flight attendant passed by inquiring if he wanted a cocktail, and Carson responded, "Vodka martini, shaken not stirred..." with a bit of a smirk.

The attendant just smiled and walked off.

In a few minutes she returned with drink in hand and said, "Here, you are Mr. Bond..."

"I always wanted to say that...", was the reply with a bit of a chuckle.

The Air Kuwaiti Boeing 757 slowly gathered power as it rolled down the runway, eventually lifting off into the mid- morning skies. Despite his many adventures, Carson was not the best of travelers. He sipped his martini and thought to himself, never again and laughed. He tried to nap and many memories came rushing in from his unconscious. He remembered being introduced and reassigned to EXECUTIVE SERVICES; his missions, the good and the bad. He found Natalia once again, only to lose her to a bullet.

At Agency HQ, Hamilton returned to with his report for the Colonel. "RIPCORD is in route to Kuwait City," announced the Chief of Staff. "Good our insurance policy...." replied the Colonel. " Now, what about our sources in the area, anything to report?"

"Nothing yet, Sir..."

48

A couple of hours had passed when Hamilton returned with news, as to the latest traffic from the Persian Gulf region," Sir, The Raven was spotted in Baghdad, four days ago."

"The Raven, in Iraq?" Was the puzzled response of Colonel Perry?

The Raven, i.e. Edgar LeClerc, was a terrorist of respect, via social media. Always sending a message via the internet or a calling card, "The RAVEN EVERMORE!"

DAY V

August 01

Kuwait City.

It was a hazy dawn as the sun spread across the Kuwaiti capital, as U.S. Military Attaché' Al Johnston walked up to his smallish grey Chevy Truck, in the parking area of his apartment complex, shared by many of the Embassy Staff.

Down the street, lying in wait was a Silver Jaguar and "the Raven." He watched as the truck passed. It was about 6:50 a.m. when the truck sped by. fifty, seventy-five, one hundred feet and the Raven pushed a button on a remote and the smallish truck erupts like that of a small atomic device, spreading destruction and chaos in the area.

The Raven quickly joined the crowd, as if he really cared. Dropped his signature card and then disappeared.

Time slowly passed as Deputy Ambassador Albert Jameson received a phone call from Hunter Thompson about Carson's pending arrival. Jameson was an old friend of Carson's days in the Naval Academy. Talking aloud the Deputy Ambassador exclaimed, "Why is that crazy fool coming here now?"

Another phone call let the Deputy Ambassador that the Military Attaché' was killed in an explosion. The Deputy Ambassador then ordered that

49

Johnston's family be relocated to the Embassy, ASAP! Trying to piece this mixture together to where it makes some level of sense. He ordered the

Military Attache's office searched and then sealed. Any information was to be brought to the Deputy Ambassador's office. His "EYES ONLY!"

The information he wanted to see was in a folder marked: Iraqi/Kuwaiti Border. It indicated a buildup of Iraqi troops along the Kuwaiti border. More reports indicated the rattling of sabers by the Iraqi Leadership. Plus, a business with a simple message," The Raven Evermore!"

The office was sealed and the Embassy prepared for the worse.

DAY VI

Message from Allah!

It was around 4:30 a.m., Kuwaiti time when the Boeing 757 landed. Carson quickly made his way through security without really noticing the welcoming contingent waiting for him. Without a hello The Deputy Ambassador handed Carson the folder from the Johnston's office and said," Get it out of here! We are about to be invaded. Langley dropped the ball on this one." A bit puzzled and dazed from jet lag Carson just say a word and followed instructions from an old friend and associate. As they made their way to the first plane available Jameson quickly briefed Carson, as to the file and events happening in the Kuwaiti Capital. Iraqi forces were invading the small nation.

Carson's plane quickly and safely escaped as troops advanced into the country!

The Captain announced over the intercom, Kuwait is being invaded by a foreign power and all we can do is pray for their safety.

May Allah be with them!

The End.

50

CODE NAME: SHADOW ORIGINS...

AUTHOR'S NOTES:

ASSIGNMENT: ANTHOLOGY is an introduction of sorts to a new generation of Political/Spy Thrillers. PROJECT: RIP (Reserve Intelligence Personnel) represents a select group of highly trained Field Operatives; officially retired, unofficially still active. Their mission is to go where American Intelligence cannot. Any failure comes in knowing that the U.S. government does not knowingly recognize them any longer as being operational!

This could be a good example of, "Plausible Deniability," associated with many Intelligence Communities of the world?

ASSIGNMENT: ANTHOLOGY(original title, ror) is a collection of short stories or assignments as an introduction to the Character of Carson Towns, CODENAME: RIPCORD, is assigned to recover (at any cost) a set of TOP SECRET Defense Department Plans: "The TRIAD DEFENSE." A question of judgement is pondered, "... In the Beginning... ". Observing a clandestine meeting at a Christmas Festival in, "The Dicken's Encounter..." and a rushed escape from Kuwait City as Iraqi Troops invade the small country.

At the moment I have currently finished the overall the rewriting this novel from the original drafts, first written some thirty years earlier, inspired, by the novels written by Ian Fleming

For I am the Student and He will always be my teacher!

Respectfully,

ROBB ROURKE

51

THE
TRIAD
DEFENSE...

AUTHOR'S NOTE

The Triad Defense was a plan designated as a rapid response scenario to any given situation in the Caribbean and South America.

Back in the 1990's plans were devised that Naval forces would be stationed along specific points within the area of the Gulf of Mexico, from Brownsville, Texas to the Florida Keys. Like most projects it was deemed pork by the new administration and cut from the budget.

Tal Johnston, a NATO currier, had just left the Norfolk, Virginia Naval Base, when his front tire exploded. What he did not know was that someone had sprayed acid on the tread of this particular tire causing it to blow at any moment.

Johnston reacted like most under similar circumstances, but lost control and crashed into a ditch, resulting in his death. The first car to pull up and assist was a Black Jaguar XL-7. The driver, Edgar Le Clerk, was often referred to as, "The Raven, "a Terrorist of International Fame.

Quickly the Raven pulled the body of the dead body of the victim from the wreckage, removed the package, and tossed in an explosive device and the walked off trying to urge the crowd to back off as true first responders' drove up. Quickly he walked through the crowd, got in his car. A turn of the keys, a shift of gears and The Raven was gone. And as the police and other first responders arrived, The Raven set off the small explosive charge and smirked," Let's make this a little more interesting."

The currier's car exploded sending the crowd into a panic. And of course, he left his calling card,

"THE RAVEN EVERMORE!"

Later police and other law enforcement confirmed that he went through security at Reagan Airport for Miami and then a charter flight to a small Island, Key Targa in the Caribbean.

In the office of Colonel Thomas Perry in Agency HEAD QUARTERS. Hamilton Jenkins', the Colonel's Chief of staff, were looking over the intelligence reports for the new President's briefing, when as of out of nowhere, the Colonel pounded fist on the desk," How in the Sam Hill did we lose those plans? "The quick response of the Chief of Staff was," Sir, two sources, Friend Raven and a Black Marketer named Francisco El Cid." And before the Colonel could respond a call from the President. Two rings and the Colonel responded," Yes Sir! We found a connection and we're on it!" Quickly the Colonel replaced the receiver back in its cradle and said, "CONTACT RIPCORD, NOW!"

On the small Island of Key Targa, Franscio El Cid was meeting with the Raven. Opening a small attaché case friend Raven, Edgar LeClerc, quickly ran his hand across the money. "Good?" El Cid inquired.

Which got a, "Very good," response from friend Raven."

A quick click of the locks and the attaché was secured and the Raven was gone.

Once again, Carson Towns was at his favorite restaurant on the Strand. Sipping his coffee sipping his morning coffee he was able to survey his surroundings as tourists crisscrossed the area.

Suddenly, a waitress handed Carson a rather large envelope and quickly disappeared, as she appeared.

A rip of the envelope and saw that he was needed home to receive a message! He paid his bill and quickly headed back to a short ride from the Strand to the Historical Home District of the Island.

Once back home, Carson reopened the envelope and read the report that discussed the murder of the NATO Currier and theft of, "the TRIAD DEFENSE."

The report also included a picture of a license plate, it was Friend Raven's. Smiling Carson couldn't help but respond, "Edgar, Edgar...."

55

The envelope also included tickets from Houston Hobby International to Miami and a connecting charter flight to Key Targa.

Over the next few hours Carson packed a small bag for this new adventure. Business as usual or will this time be different?

Carson's flight, an Air Florida 727 landed on time in Miami. He then made his way through security and then over to the Air Caribbean Charter flights Counter. A quick check in, a short wait and the flight was ready for takeoff. As he walked onto the tarmac Carson was directed to a Cessna Turbo Prop being fueled up. Loaded his gear and climbed in. The pilot climbed aboard after he ran through his final pre-flight check.

The Cessna quickly taxied to the airstrip and took off for their flight to Key Targa.

Upon landing the Cessna was met by a small welcoming committee of two jeeps one driver and well- armed guard in each. Once exited from the small plane Carson was patted down for any possible weapons, of which he did not carry this time.

Carson was coolly escorted to the second jeep. As he walked toward the jeep Carson made to take note of the surroundings, which consisted of two steel buildings that looked rather new. The immediate area consisted of what looked like a newly paved runway.

Finally, the jeeps arrived at a lavish mansion which was El Cid's private estate. Carson remembered El Cid's obsession with American Movies and Television. The mansion, itself looked like it was, "Tara, from Gone with the Wind." As he looked at the mansion, one thought crossed his mind, "Would he encounter, Scarlett O'Hara?"

56

Waiting at the front door was El Cid's Number 2, Fernando Rameriz. After a shove by the guard, Carson turned to respond, with clinched fist and quickly changed his mind as he saw guns pointed in his direction and replied, "That anyway to treat a guest?" "You are not a guest yet, Mr. Towns," responded El Cid's number 2. "And when do I become a guest?" Then with one motion Rameriz escorted Carson in, "When you enter, Mr. Towns!"

Again, Carson made note of his surroundings as thoughts of Rhett Butler at the base of the grand stairs awaiting the arrival of Scarlett...

"Say, when do, I meet with...." Carson asked. Assuming the question Rameriz already had a prepared answer, "You don't ask, for he will call on you, when he's ready. Now, is a time to rest and relax." And on that note Rameriz then escorted Carson to his room, atop the stairs.

What Carson did not realize that from another entrance way a startled Natalia Krorski, came to a sudden and complete stop, as she acted as if she'd just seen a ghost. Natalia, a member of the Third Department, First Directorate of the KGB, otherwise referred to as State Defense Directorate. What no one realized

was that Carson and Natalia had a brief affair when both were assigned to their perspective embassies in Paris. They fell in love and abruptly torn apart. "What is it, Natalia? You look like startled you," inquired her partner on this particular assignment. "It's nothing, just the decadent feel of American Propaganda!" There she stood thinking of her time with Carson. Six months of passion and no politics. They parted out of sadness and the same politics it would appear to possibly bring them together again!

57

In his suite, Carson, unpacked his small bag and quickly removing his android phone, a few taps on the keypad and proceeded to sweep the room for listening devices. Now time

relax. His meeting will occur later that evening and now it was time to relax. Flopping on the bed Carson was soon asleep. Suddenly as the power nap started it was interrupted by a phone call summoning him down stairs for his meeting.

Just as he felt asleep the landline phone rang startling Carson out of a relaxing sleep. Carson in picking up the receiver was instructed to prepare for dinner with Senor El Cid. So, a quick refresher, new deodorant, and comb through his hair and all Carson would need was his coat, as he awaited his escort.

As Carson and his escort the grand hallways and into the dining hall, he couldn't help but notice how remarkably similar to the Movie,"Tara!" This should make Ted Turner jealous!

Upon arrival in the dining hall Carson heard a loud, boastful voice," Come in and have a seat, Senor Towns..." It was Francisco El Cid. He was a man in his late fifties, and what

Carson could easily describe as, "...Liking to hear himself, Talk!" Carson had a brief memory flash as he often said that of his Dad.

"Senor El Cid, I am truly honored to be a guest here in your beautiful Mansion." "Ah, so you like, 'Casa El Tara?' I often wonder might Senor Turner might think if he knew of its existence?" This comment was followed by a hearty laugh by both men.

"Now we eat! A meal fit for a King..." ordered the host as Carson was shown his seat at the table. The conversation centered back to "Casa El Tara," as both men discussed the positives and negatives of this grand movie.

Carson then asked, "Did you ever see the sequel: Scarlett?"

58

Sitting back in his chair, El Cid had a scowl on his face, that quickly as he commented on the problems "Senor Dalton, was no Rhett Butler as he was no James Bond..."

The meal was grand, and up to what El Cid described as a meal, "...fit for a King!"

Both men quickly rose from the table as servants came to remove the dinner dishes. They were escorted to El Cid's private billiard room and library. The room was just as grand as the mansion itself. The books were all first editions from Shakespeare to Poe, to the likes of Tom Clancy, and Stephen King.

The pool table was regulation is size, but looked to grand to be found in just a pool hall.

"Well, Senor Towns, as to why you are here?" inquired El Cid.

"You have something that I have been asked to try and negotiate to get back?"

Walking over the rack of pool cues, El Cid remarked, " I had a feeling Senor, that was why you were here," as he grabbed two cues. Tossing one to Carson, El Cid added, "You up for a game of 8 -ball, Senor as we discuss *your bid." Racking up the balls Carson replied, "You break!"*

With the objective to sink the 8-ball last this game of elimination began. El Cid broke the racked pool balls sending two into the far left and right pockets. Setting up his next shot two more balls landed in their respective pockets. Then out of the blue a servant walked in with their after-dinner coffee and cigars.

The servant accidently bumped El Cid causing him to miss his shot. Now it was Carson's turn. First ball went in the pocket leaving 3-balls including the prized 8-ball. Next shot another was sunk, leaving just two.

59

Pausing for a moment, Carson couldn't help from noticing that El Cid was boiling mad at the servant, but was trying not to show it in front of business. Carson made an interesting move by sinking the 8-ball instead of his intended target of the 4-ball.

Claiming victory, El Cid was able to regain his composure and cool. Extending his hand El Cid remarked," You, Senor played a great game, but in the end... Home field advantage is a real bitch!" with a big smile on his face.

Then walking Carson over to his desk El Cid, commented, " Now down to business..."

The two men talked until the wee hours of the next morning discussing the business at hand, "The Triad Defense!"

"And how do I know if what you have is real or not?" inquired Carson. "Senor Towns, when it comes to business...I discuss business!" El Cid remarked as he leaned in Carson's direction.

Feeling victorious, El Cid ordered a servant to bring beer and limes for them to drink. The servant returned with a tray with three beers and a bowl of limes. "Are you expecting company?" asked a curious Carson. "Si, Senor! Your competition from Moscow, will be here shortly!" was the curt response.

Within a couple of minutes the door opened and Colonel Boris Rosnik of the Directorate of State Security. "K.G. B., right?" Carson inquired. "American!" was the response. "Well, you two I thought it might make things interesting to let the competition meet each other!" "Senor, El Cid, I must protest. I was debriefed as to this being a private business session between myself and you, not this American?"

"And I like you, too...." Carson retorted. This was followed by a quick shove as the scenario was starting to show signs of

getting out of hand, when a blast from Carson's past entered the room. Natalia Korski, his former lover, from his time stationed

at the Embassy in Paris, France. Their eyes met as if time and distance did not exist! "Colonel, is there something wrong?" Natalia inquired, as she continued to stare at Carson."No, nothing is wrong?"

Both El Cid and Colonel Rosnik couldn't help from noticing that Carson and Natalia just couldn't take their eyes off each other. "Do you know each other, Senior Towns?", asked a rather curious El Cid. "We met once, in Paris," was Carson's response.

The beer was offered and business began. El Cid began the process, "I have in my possession a top- secret document, outlining U.S. Naval plans to defend the Caribbean and Gulf of Mexico. " and then produced a small thumb drive. "Now, I will let each of you bid for this information over the next couple of days. You can examine it on a limited basis. And then you will submit a bid in Gold!" announced El Cid The Russian Colonel began to sweat and Carson's only remarks were a shrug of the shoulders and, "Impressive?"

"And as I say good night, to the winner, I will pass on to you one thumb drive and any accompanying Computer links." responded El Cid. On that note El Cid quickly exited the room followed by security.

She looked in his direction, but Carson was already walking through the door and to his room with his guard in tow. Colonel Roznik and Natalia were also escorted back to their room, with the good Colonel lecturing Natalia as to how well she knew Carson Towns?

61

Back in his room, Carson did a brief scan for listening devices. He always remembered chewing gum could wind up in the darnedist places. A couple of slices chewed enough did the trick. He then showered and prepared for bed. He couldn't get to sleep right away, as he kept thinking of Natalia...

Finally, sleep took a hold of him, yet he dreamt of Natalia; their apartment in Paris, the passion they shared and the heartbreak he felt when he discovered that show was gone!

Carson, arose about mid-morning and quickly decided for a quick run. His route took him the length of the estate. He also made note of pathway that seemed to be heavily guarded. "Interesting, very interesting..." thinking aloud as he ran by.

Carson would later find out that path led to El Cid's private office and warehouse. As a matter of fact, El Cid was giving Colonel Rosnik a quick study of the documents.

"Well, Colonel it seems the American is making a good impression and sales pitch for the product in question. Can your President do better?" And," Senor, my superiors feel that it would be in your best interests, not to disappoint them!"

"Ah..." was El Cid's response.

Carson discovered the estate pool and quickly decided take a swim. As quick as he could get his sneakers off they were tossed aside, and as he tried to pull his sweaty shirt off a familiar voice remarked, " I never imagined you hot and bothered..." and started laughing. Turning around Carson replied, not knowing who it was that made the comment. It was Natalia, still as beautiful as the day they met in Paris. They just stood there staring at each other waiting for someone to blink. Finally, Natalia broke the ice and asked, "Is this any way to treat an old friend?" "No, it's not as he walked over to her and then directed her to one of the lounge chairs, where they began talking and remembering things like they never parted. Carson leaned toward Natalia and smirked, "I want to get something off my chest..."

" Typical decadent American response, and that's why I fell in love with you!" was her response as she looked lovingly into his eyes. This very soon followed by a very passionate embrace!

In the distance a member of the Security Staff made a call to El Cid notifying him of what was happening poolside! A few clicks of the keypad and a live feed from the security monitor clicked poolside viewing Carson and Natalia embracing. "Well, Senor Rosnik, it appears the American has an edge on you," announced El Cid, as he turned the monitor in the direction of the Russian Colonel. It could be said that the good Colonel's anger level was almost to that of the old crimson flag of the former Soviet Union! "NO, NO, !!!" he shouted as he left El Cid's office. He quickly grabbed the first jeep he could find, driving like, "a bat out of hell!"

Rosnik quickly and abruptly came to a stop near the pool, almost flipping it over! A turn of the key and he jumped out charging the twosome, shouting in Russian. "you know, my dear your associate need to take a tranquilizer, so he can calm down," Carson quipped. Quickly, Natalia rose and stood at attention for Rosnik was her superior. Grabbing her by the arm Rosnik slapped Natalia across the mouth and Carson quickly responded with a right cross to the chin sending the Colonel into a row of poolside chairs. Quickly, Rosnik was up brushing himself off as Natalia was in Carson's arms. Grabbing her Rosnik responded, "come Natalia, I will deal with you later. As for you American your turn will come!" "Go for it... "was Carson's response.

63

And from his monitor, El Cid was enjoying the jousting among the competition. Yet, he found it interesting as to the reactions between Natalia and Carson...

Poolside, Carson just shook off the events of a prior few minutes before and took a swim. As everything on what appeared, on this rather smallish island and its accessories were a bit to luxurious for Carson's taste! As he swam a few laps he pondered his next moves?

About midnight Carson was able to jimmy the lock on an outside window that allowed him the ability to quickly blend into the background. After a few minutes of getting a lay of the land Carson quietly and quickly made his way along the dark pathway he discovered earlier, and then again into the bushes as he heard footsteps coming from behind. It was Natalia also dressed in similar night attire. Grabbing her from behind, Carson reacts, "What in the Sam Hill are you doing here?" Turning slowly but passionately Natalia, putting her arms around Carson's neck responded, "I always liked your rear movements!" "And this is not the time or place for fun and games, darling. I'm not 007" "Your, right your no Sean Connery!" she replied with a chuckle. A Pause and then Carson responded, "Again, what are you doing out here?" "Following you! I made a mistake once in Paris, not again!" Which was followed by a long and passionate kiss. Taking a breath, Carson responded, "I needed to hear that, but I need to get that file!"

Grabbing his hand Natalia acted as a guide in the dark as they made their way down the dark pathway. Suddenly the sounds of a large truck came rumbling toward them. A quick jump in to the bushes as the truck approached. Another quick move and the twosome were running after the truck jumping on for the ride into an underground warehouse of a large scale

64

Once again Carson exited the back of the truck as soon as it came to a stop. He tried to convince Natalia to wait but he had forgotten how stubborn she was...

They decided that the best route was to move along the background and blend in. This problem was solved when Carson discovered a rather good hiding place, a stack of crates marked uniforms. Quickly getting into two uniforms Carson and Natalia were blending into the background. They followed the direction signs on the walls that led to the offices on another level. They quickly found El Cid's private office and after pulling out a small black wallet from his pocket, revealed a set of tool picks and in a matter of minutes the door was open. Once inside Carson made a quick survey of the office, while Natalia served as lookout. Pulling out one of three special thumb drives Carson quickly able to download and forward, "the Triad Defense," file back to Langley and CIA. The same thumb drive was also designed to erase all files on the computer that was being used at the time, basically frying the hard drive.

Quickly the door was locked and Carson and Natalia made their way to the hiding place they found moments before. Little did they realize that Colonel Roznik was shadowing them and caught them in their hiding place. "Well, American you lose. Hand over the thumb drive or I will kill your lover!"

There was no choice, so Carson slowly pulled out a thumb drive, this on containing a small explosive charge. In passing it over Carson triggered the timer long enough for Rosnik to drop the thumb drive in his front pants pocket. "Well, American, like I said, you lose." And as he was about to pull the trigger the explosive charged went off catching the startled Rosnik completely off guard tossing him backwards into the crates behind him. Grabbing Natalia, Carson remarked, "I bet that will leave a mark?"

65

As he slipped the thumb drive back into his pocket Carson noticed a box marked c-4 explosives. Quickly Carson ordered Natalia to gather an ample supply of c-4 and timers and they needed a diversion if they wanted to escape. Quickly Carson placed some of the c-4 in the hiding area where the remains of Colonel Rosnik were laid out under a stack of crates. Carson set the timer for two minutes. Just enough time to get out of the immediate explosion zone and where they could maybe plant a few more surprises.

The first detonation came and chaos began to reign. Carson quickly set up another charge as Natalia quickly hotwired a nearby jeep. El Cid, quickly notified and in route as he and his driver actually passed Carson and Natalia as they roared by. A sudden stop and turn of the vehicle and El Cid and driver were in hot pursuit. Carson response to the hail of bullets was to drop a timer attached to some c-4 but of course the timer was set for about 7 seconds. Just enough time to blow up the front of the on-charging vehicle.

With the Airstrip insight Carson and Natalia headed for the first Airplane available." Can you hotwire a plane?" He asked already the answer. "Yes, "was the response with a sense *of Authority. In a few minutes the plane was rolling down the airstrip and security finally showed up. El Cid even was vowing vengeance for the events of the night.*

Natalia leaned over and kissed Carson on the Cheek and remarked," So decadent Mr. Bond, but I love it!" "Which one?"

The inquiring mind asked. "Comrade Moore, for now...." was the reply followed a hearty laugh and feeling free for once in her life.

*Glancing over at Natalia, Carson remarked,"
When I first saw you the other night, it was
just like all the hate did not exist!"*

*Natalia, leaned over and kissed him on the
cheek. They were able to land in key Largo,
where they able to rent a car and drove to
Miami, where they hopped a plane to
Houston and then Galveston.*

*At Langley, in Colonel Perry's office,
Hamilton rushed in shouting, "He made it!
He made it, Sir!" As the Colonel was about to
respond the printer started up. It was a print
out of*

"The Triad Defense."

*"RIPCORD, good work, "was the Colonel's
response. "Good Work." Hamilton then
added that Carson had a Russian woman
with him. Sitting back in his chair, the
Colonel ponder a thought aloud,*

"Could it be? "

"Could it be what, Sir?" inquired a puzzled Chief of Staff. "When he was assigned to the American Embassy in Paris he met and fell in love with a then Soviet Operative named Natalia Korskia. And upon finding out about the romance I had a little talk with her to convince her it would not be in either of their interests that their budding romance be allowed to grow! And he doesn't know that she gave birth to their son eight months later!" I made sure it was kept quiet and I made sure that when it was time to bring about EXECUTIVE: SERVICES, he would be my first choice!"

"And now he will find out about his son, left back in Russia. Yes, and I have been keeping tabs on him ever since!" the Colonel added. "You are rather fond of RIPCORD, Sir?"

"Yes, He's like a son to me!" then as to point a finger of authority, the Colonel added, "And you will never tell him!"

Shaking his head with approval and respect Hamilton quickly exited his superiors' office.

Over the next couple of weeks Carson and Natalia reminisced of their love as if it was yesterday. They dined along the seawall, and walked along the Strand Historical District. Suddenly one morning as they were strolling along the opening store fronts of the Strand they did not notice a car slowly cruising behind them. It was the Raven, in the back seat. All of a sudden, a shot rang out striking Natalia in the back, mortally wounding her last words were of their son Nicholas, "He knows of you. He must know his Father!" and life past the afterlife. Carson was beside himself and confused for the first time in his life. All he could do is hold her in his arms, as tightly as he could as a means of maybe healing her.

The Car sped off. The police and paramedics arrived but to no avail as Natalia was gone...

A couple of days later was the funeral, it was quiet and peaceful. Some of Carson's former associates, from Company days were there. Even Colonel Perry attended, but from a distance.

Later, Carson arrived at his Historical District home, with thoughts of wanting to be anywhere but Galveston, didn't realize that Colonel Perry was in the room waiting for him. "Well, what are you plans, RIPCORD?"

"WHAT?" Carson barked back at his mentor and boss. "Are you going after El Cid?" "YES!" was Carson's response. "My next question is of Vengeance or Duty?" A stare of hate was Carson's response. Colonel Perry then rose from his chair and started to leave when he paused and said," When you can answer my question, the assignment is yours! My sympathies for your loss. As to your son, let me know what I can do!" and then quickly exited to an awaiting car.

Moscow; the office of the Russian President. He arrived to find a single yellow rose with a copy of the funeral program for Natalia's Service.

A note was attached and it read:

She died in the line of fire Comrade!

Signed,

A Tall Texan!

The End

In the Beginning.......
CODE NAME: RIPCORD
WITHIN THE SHADOWS

Over the next couple of weeks Carson and Natalia reminisced about their love as if it were yesterday. They toured the Strand and ate at the famous Seafood Restaurants' of the Island.

Then suddenly one morning as they were strolling along the opening store fronts of the Strand they did not notice a car slowly cruising behind them. It was the Raven, in the back seat. All of a sudden, a shot rang out striking Natalia in the back, mortally wounding her last words were of their son Nicholas, "He knows of you. He must know his Father!" and life past the afterlife. Carson was beside himself and confused for the first time in his life. All he could do is hold her in his arms, as tightly as he could as a means of maybe healing her.

A couple of days later the funeral, it was quiet and peaceful. nds and associates, from his Company days were in attendance, but at a distance.

Later at his house in the Historical District of Galveston, with his thoughts were of anywhere, but home, Carson did not realize that the Colonel was there, waiting for him! "Well, Plans?" He asked. "What the Hell?" Carson barked back at his mentor and boss. "Duty or Vengeances?" questioned the Colonel. A stare of Hate was Carson's response. Then, the Colonel abruptly rose from his chair started to leave, paused to say, "As to El Cid, when you can answer my question, the assignment is yours! As to your son, let me see what I can pull out of my hat..." and then he briskly exited to an awaiting car.

In Moscow, the Presidential Palace. The President arrived at his office to find a single Yellow Rose with a copy of the funeral

program for Natalia. Puzzled the Russian President read an additional note:

72.

She Died in, "The Line of Fire!" Comrade!

A TALL TEXAN!

One year later....

As the sun rose over the Gulf of Mexico, Carson Towns stood above the wavering surf. A tear came to his eyes as he remembered it was the first anniversary of Natalia's death... A life and memories revisited and shattered by a single bullet. Looking at the locket that she once wore, and the two pictures of Natalia and Nicholas their son! Many thoughts and questions were pondered in those brief moments.

As suddenly as he retraced memories of the past, reality flashed him back to the present as his cellphone chimed one of his many James Bond ringtones. "The competition, "he often smirked as he read the confirmation message concerning a floral order and delivery at the cemetery.

Quickly, he jumped in to his rebuilt 1979 Pontiac Sunbird, fondly nicknamed, "The Maroon Menace." A turn of the key, a shift of the gears and Carson was headed home for a quick shower and then to the cemetery. Memories of that first encounter. A rainy day, a chance meeting at a small café on the Left Bank in Paris, France. A botched attempt of speaking French that brought a, "Well, I hope your English is better..." response as

Natalia offered him a chair, next to her, an alliance of love, which lasted six months.

It was Christmas when Carson walked into the small apartment they shared, secretly. Yet, this day was different for Natalia had moved out. What he didn't know was that she was hiding in the

bedroom closet. He left heart broken. She left with a secret, which in seven months became their son Nicholas.

A quick turn on to Broadway Avenue and then down 23rd street and home, a Victorian style home in the middle of the Island's Historical District

73

A shift of Gears, a turn of the key and Carson headed in. Another turn of a key and he walked in.

In Langley, Virginia, at Agency Headquarters, Colonel Perry and Hamilton Jenkins, Chief of Staff, were discussing

New reports had recently surfaced on the whereabouts Francisco El Cid. In leaning back in his chair, Colonel Perry just happened to glance at the calander on his desk and inquired, "Is this date correct?" Puzzled Hamilton responded, "Sir?" Today's date, That Russian Girl. One year ago, she died in RIPCORD'S arms. "The Colonel responded. With a sigh Hamilton added his regrets as he also briefly forgot the memory of that time.

"Sir, with these reports of El Cid, are you planning to assign RIPCORD?" inquired Hamilton. "That's a good question. "A very good question!" It would be a question that Colonel Perry had been pondering for a very long while!

THE END

DUTY
OR
VENGEANCE?

THE

ASSIGNMENT;

TRACK DOWN AND OBSERVE OPERATIONS OF ONE FRANCO EL CID IN SOUTH AMERICA!

The assignment was plain and simple, Franco El Cid had relocated his operational base to the jungles of Peru; gather intelligence and report back via usual channels.

Carson, knowing that he and his fellow, "EXECUTIVE SERVICE, OPERATIVES," would be denied by Washington if anything went south, while on assignment; gather intelligence, "RIGHT?' This was his chance to seek vengeance for Natalia's murder ordered by Franco El Cid!

Just as Carson's lyft ride arrived he quickly took a couple of notes, like contacts, etc. and shredded all assignment printouts!

As he gazed at the passing landscape, his thoughts began to waver between his anger for Natalia dying from a bullet meant for him and his sense of duty to the job at hand! The anger, he could still feel just a couple of years after the fact. But now he had other factors to consider as important factors indirectly to the assignment: His son Nicholas, by Natalia, and now Mia, his second chance at love. The ride to Hobby Airport seemed to be longer than usual but it still took just an hour and a half. A quick tip to the driver and Carson walked into the Terminal.

After passing through security Carson waited for his flight to be announced, and once again the thought of the assignment:" A Call to duty or an act of revenge?" slowly took over intertwined with thoughts of Natalia as he re-imagined the events of that particular day!

Suddenly the announcement of his flight was to board. The Boeing 737 jumbo jet started to fill quickly as Carson found his seat. The hatch was sealed and the plane was taxied across the runway.

77

A pause for final instructions and then the jumbo jet rolled down the runway and into the mid-morning skies.

The flight would take a good portion of the day allowing Carson's mind to wonder once again from the thought of killing El Cid or doing his duty! His first thoughts were that of Natalia, as she died in his arms. There was a peaceful look on her face as she passed into an everlasting sleep.

She knew the risks of the job they shared as well as Carson did. She also knew the love they shared for those brief moments on Galveston. A sense of calm and dare one say relief as every time he thought of her he could imagine her beauty and her touch. Yet, he also sensed a streak of guilt despite the fact that part of the profession they aspired to exist was filled with danger!

At Agency Head Quarters in Langley, Virginia Hamilton responded to a call from The Colonel. Hamilton took his usual place opposite his superior. The Colonel appeared a bit out of sorts giving Hamilton an opportunity to inquire. "Hamilton, I did not realize this is the third anniversary of that Russian girl's murder, and I sent RIPCORD after El Cid. I hope that he does his job!" "Sir, you gave him the assignment and RIPCORD will do what is right, as long as the job is done!" was the response. "Hamilton, your right he didn't have to take the assignment, but he knows his sense of Duty!" commented the Colonel.

Not far from the Manu National Park located in the region of Madre And Cusco of Peru, El Cid stood on a balcony of his treetop complex. It was a panoramic view of the Amazon River. He enjoyed the view, but was concerned about the security over the entire complex. He was having issues with the nearby tribes, who hunted in the area. Some were caught and fed to the Caiman's (Large Alligator speciese linked to the Amazon River Region. Other's he let escape to keep the tribes quiet!

78

" Senior Cid, Senior Cid," Yelled his new head of Security, Miguel Santos. "There is news of Carson Towns, Senior Cid!" Hearing this El Cid could only respond, "I'm not worried about Carson Towns, not worried at all!" Clapped his hands together and turned back to his panoramic view of the Amazon River basin.

THE END?

BACKLASH- POSSIBLE...

At CIA Head Quarters- Langley, Virginia

The Colonel, summoned Hamilton that he wanted to discuss something with him.

Hamilton quickly entered and took his spot opposite the Colonel. "RIPCORD?" he inquired. Pounding his fist on the desk, the Colonel responded with an almost guilty sense of anger in his voice, "Damn it Man! You know who I'm talking about!"

Now leaning back in his chair Hamilton replied, with non responsive look on his face, " Sir, I have been your Chief of Staff of many years, and this is the first time that I feel like questioning your actions, but Sir, RIPCORD knows the assignment, duty first!"

With a scowl of a stare the Colonel responded, "You have been with Me a longtime, Ham and I respect your opinions! And yes, Carson knows the risks of the job at hand! This just seems different! There seems to be something wrong, about the mission as a whole!"

There was a sudden pause and then Hamilton replied, "The Russian Girl, Sir! Remember! I believe that her name was

Natalia? They also share a child together, Sir"

"Oh, my God the Russian Girl, reflected the Colonel. And followed up by asking, " And the child, Nicholas? How old is he now?" " Latest intell... has young Nicholas about 21 years of age and living with his Maternal Grandfather, just outside Moscow," was the response from Hamilton.

Then the Colonel inquired, "Can we get Carson's son and his Grandfather here and have him waiting in Texas when he arrives?" A bit stunned Hamilton paused a bit then reacted, "I'll get on that right away, Sir..." and quickly exited from the Colonel's office.

81

Once back in his office, Hamilton quickly made calls to contacts at the Department of State and Defense. The objective was to seek a solution that would bring Nicholas and his Grandfather to the States.

It is early evening in Lima, Peru as the Jumbo Jet carrying Carson Towns landed at the International Airport . Carson made his way through airport security and was met by an old associate Tom Smith. Tom was a retired field, (and yes, filed operatives do retire) and Peru was as far away as he could get! Carson,"What in the Hell are you doing here?" "I needed to get away from it all!" was the response. A raised eyebrow and Tom Replied, " and I thought you missed me?" This was followed by a laugh that could share. Tom helped Carson run through Customs and they collected Carson's gear and they left in Tom's Pontiac Sunbird. As they drove Tom decided to ask why Carson came to Peru," So, what brings you to my neck of the woods? and I want the truth, no B.S. !" I need some help and you are the local expert on the area, that I know!" "In other words, the Old Bastard, sent you?" A self-answer to his original question! "I thought he was dead by now..." Tom added!

"There have been times that I wondered if he would ever die," commented Carson. "He's not human! That's why he'll never die! Hamilton is actually in charge and he has the old man running by batteries!" Again they laughed. "So, where are we going?" asked Carson. There's this bar where we can talk and you look like you need to talk to someone!" was Tom's response.

They drove into downtown Lima and came across a small bar called, "A bit South East of the Border." Looking at the Bar name Carson replied a bit sarcastically ," A bit South East of the Border?" "And what are you worrying about the food isn't bad and the drink are worse!" was the response from an old friend with a silly smile on his face.

So, Carson *and Tom Smith pulled into a parking space and then the bar, itself! Tom ordered a couple of beers and started to pump Carson for info as to why he was in Peru. Carson told his friend about Natalia, and Nicholas. He gave his friend around about response to why he was really there! "I still think, he's an old Bastard!" Tom Stated!*

In his tree house complex El Cid was looking over the reports on Carson Town; when he landed and who met him at the airport! "So, Carson Towns what brings you to Peru, if I don't already know?" remarked El Cid.

THE END:

FOR NOW/TBD!

EPILOGUE

HERO'S

Who are our Hero's?

We each will have our own criteria and respect for those who we define as Hero's! Being a History Buff, my Hero's come via their achievement in History; Franklin D. Roosevelt, a man in a wheelchair, that at this country's lowest moment showed us how to, "Once Again Stand Tall!"

I had two uncles' that served in WWII; One in Italy, and One in the Pacific, they are on my Hero's List.

Another Name on that list is that of Ian Fleming, the Spy Master of Literature's Most Celebrated Spy, James Bond.

Ian Fleming served British and Allied Intelligence during WWII as an Intelligence Officer. Through his experiences resulted in the adventures of 007.

I look to Mr. Fleming, not just as a hero, but that of a Mentor/Teacher. He built the framework for the action/adventure genre!

CODE NAME: SHADOW ORIGINS

Is my first attempt at writing a Spy novel. This is also my way to pay respect to, "A HERO!"

A CHALLENGE OF THIS BOOK;

Like most books that are fictional accounts of storytelling, I believe that a lot of stories have forgotten one thing; imaginations. Imagination allows us to enjoy the tale and get a sense of the action and suspense. Today, there are many ways to read a book, but how many ways are there, to really enjoy the read?

So, I challenge the readers' of this book, and since there are no physical descriptions of any of the characters, use your imagination and describe each character as you see them!

And do send me your thoughts

To the following email and I will try and respond as quick as possible:

002rourker@gmail.com.

ENJOY THE READ!

Robb Rourke

DOSSIER:

My name is Robb Rourke. (and I really love the fact that this particular Word Program says my last name is misspelled, LOL)

I am a 5th Generation Texan and (BOI) Born on the Island of Galveston, Texas. I have a daughter and if anyone is curious, "So, Ladies I am single!"(LOL)

CODE NAME: RIPCORD

Will return

In

CHECKMATE

tbd

Made in the USA
Columbia, SC
29 January 2023

11184829R00093